the BUNNY BUNCH FAMILY

by SUNNY GRIFFIN

ILLUSTRATED BY ESTHER KENNEDY

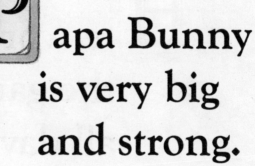

P apa Bunny
is very big
and strong.

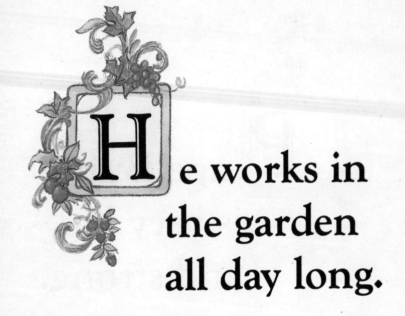

He works in the garden all day long.

Mama Bunny
is as busy
as can be.

She cooks
and feeds
our family.

Sister Bunny
draws and
paints
each day.

She goes to school to learn and to play.

Brother Bunny rides his big red bike to school.

E veryday he goes to the Bunnyville swimming pool.

Baby Bunny is held and loved by everyone.

He eats and
sleeps and
has lots
of fun.

Grandma and Grandpa Bunny are special, too.

So come and visit...

...we all
like
y<u>ou</u>!